# LOVE

BY **Stacy McAnulty**

ILLUSTRATED BY
**Joanne Lew-Vriethoff**

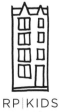

RP | KIDS
PHILADELPHIA

Running Press Kids
Hachette Book Group
1290 Avenue of the Americas, New York, NY 10104
www.runningpress.com/rpkids
@RP_Kids

Printed in China

First Edition: December 2018

Published by Running Press Kids, an imprint of Perseus Books, LLC, a subsidiary of Hachette Book Group, Inc.
The Running Press Kids name and logo is a trademark of the Hachette Book Group.

The Hachette Speakers Bureau provides a wide range of authors for speaking events.
To find out more, go to www.hachettespeakersbureau.com or call (866) 376-6591.

The publisher is not responsible for websites (or their content) that are not owned by the publisher.

Print book cover and interior design by T. L. Bonaddio.

Library of Congress Control Number: 2016963266

ISBNs: 978-0-7624-6212-4 (hardcover), 978-0-7624-6213-1 (ebook), 978-0-7624-9254-1 (ebook), 978-0-7624-9255-8 (ebook)

1010

10  9  8  7  6  5  4  3  2  1

For Kristen—S. M.

For Stacy, Teresa, and Julie,
family, much LOVE—J. L. V.

Love is . . .

a fancy dinner.

Love needs
special presents.

And designer greeting cards.

Love calls for bouquets of flowers.

And must have the finest chocolate.

Love sounds
like poetry.

Love comes in the shape of a heart.

And sparkles like diamonds.

Love happens
at first sight.

And needs the tightest hugs.

Love deserves to be shouted from the rooftops.

Because nothing else matters without . . .